THE
LITTLE FIRE ENGINE

THE
LITTLE FIRE ENGINE

LOIS LENSKI

Random House New York

Fireman Small has a
little fire engine.
He keeps it in
the firehouse.

The little fire engine is a pumper.
A pumper uses its engine to pump the water.
The truck carries black suction hose on one side,
    and a ladder on the other.
The fire hose is in the body of the truck.

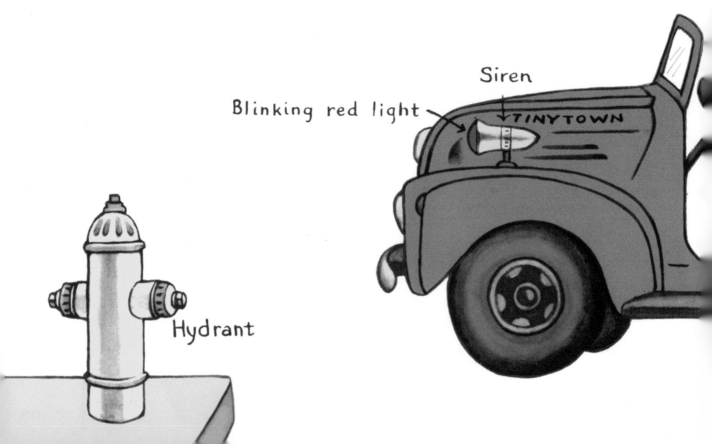

Siren

Blinking red light

TINYTOWN

Hydrant

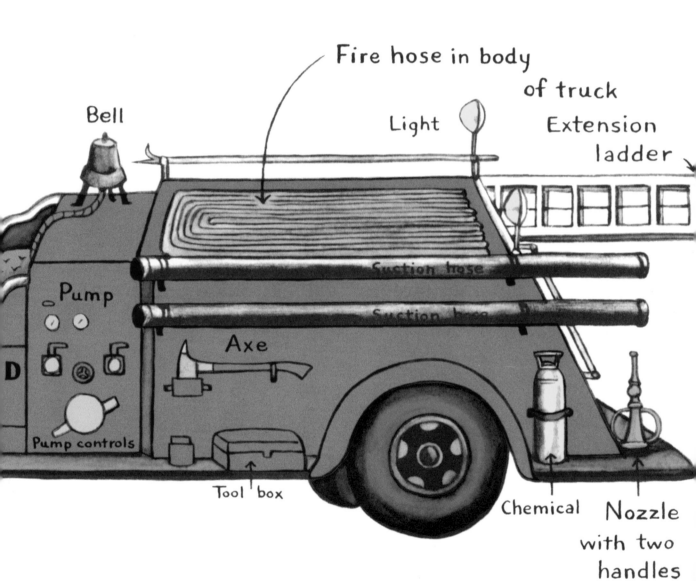

Fire hose in body of truck

Bell

Light

Extension ladder

Pump

Axe

D

Suction hose

Suction hose

Pump controls

Tool box

Chemical

Nozzle with two handles

Fireman Small sleeps upstairs
in the firehouse.
Ding-ding! Ding-ding-ding!
goes the alarm bell.
"Two-three! Fire at Church and
Summer streets!" calls Fireman Small.
He jumps out of bed quickly.

Fireman Small slides down
the pole.

Fireman Small puts on his helmet
and rubber coat.
He jumps on the seat and starts the engine.
M-m-m-m-m-mum!
The other firemen come running.
Tinker, the fire dog, comes running, too!

The firehouse doors
 swing open.
The little fire engine
 moves into the street.
Nang, nang,
 nang, nang
 goes the bell.

The little fire engine goes faster and faster.
All the cars pull over to the curb
    to let it pass.
Nang, nang, nang, nang goes the bell.
Ooo-o-WEEE-ooo-oo-o-o
    goes the siren.

The little fire engine turns the corner
into Main Street.
Nang, nang, nang, nang goes the bell.
Ooo-o-WEEE-ooo goes the siren.
All the people stop to look.
Where is the fire?

The little fire engine comes to Church and
Summer streets. The corner house is on fire.
Smoke is coming out of doors and windows.

The little fire engine
slows down by the hydrant
and drops off the hose.

The firemen unload the hose
from the truck.
They lay the hose to the fire.

Fireman Small
screws the nozzle
on the end of the hose.
The other end
goes to the pumper.

The suction hose goes from the
pumper to the hydrant.

"Go inside the house!"
  shouts Fireman Small.
"Find out where
  the fire is!"
The firemen take pikes
and axes and march in
  at the door.

"Start the pump!" orders Fireman Small.
"Turn the water on!"
The pump starts pumping. *Swish!* The water
comes shooting out of the nozzle.
The family carry sofa, lamps, tables, and
chairs out of the house.

A fireman calls out the window:
"The fire is around
   the kitchen chimney!"
Fireman Small and his men
take the hose to the kitchen.
   They rush in at the
      back door.

"Oh, look!" Everybody looks.
A little girl is standing at the upstairs window.
She has a kitten in her arms.
"Mama!" she calls.
"Stay right where you are," answers her mother.
"Fireman Small is coming.
He will bring you down."

"Get the ladder!" orders Fireman Small.
The firemen run and bring the ladder.
"Run it up! Hurry!"

Fireman Small climbs up the ladder.
He lifts the little girl out of the window
and carries her down.
She runs to her father and mother.
"Hooray!" shout the people.

Fireman Small goes up the ladder again.
He takes his axe.
The fire is in the attic now.
He chops a hole in the roof.

The firemen take the hose up the ladder.
Fireman Small squirts water down
into the hole. *Z-z-z-z-z!*
White clouds of steam rise up.
The flames die down.

"The fire is out!" shouts Fireman Small.
"Stop the pump! Turn off the water!"
The firemen do what they are told.
They put everything back in the truck.
Tinker is still waiting in his seat!

"The fire is over!" says Fireman Small.
"Move right back in again!"
The family carry their sofa, lamps,
tables, and chairs into the house.

"The fire is over!"
says Fireman Small.
"Let's go!"
He drives slowly
back to the
firehouse.

And
that's all
about
Fireman
Small !